KID COACH

Rob Justus

PAGE
STREET
KIDS

Kid Coach knows a thing or two about winning.
He takes couch potatoes and mashes them into champions.

Just ask Dad—**couch potato extraordinaire!**
But the path from potato to champion is not easy.

It starts with **little** challenges

and **small** wins.

And builds to **bigger** challenges

and **major** wins.

Today Kid Coach and Dad will wrangle . . .

BALD guys,

(and a scary guy with tattoos of
BIG, BAD, BALD guys!)
in the grandest arena
of them all—

He flips
the Flamingo.

He chops
the Cheetah.

Dad racks up **win,**

after **win,**

after **win.**

No one can escape his signature move:

The Tater
TANGLER!

But as the day goes on, Kid Coach notices something.

Dad starts to dance a *little* too long,

celebrate a *little* too much,

he won't
EVEN
shake hands!

Dad could be making new friends, but instead
BIG GUYS are sad guys,
BAD GUYS are mad guys,
(bald guys are still bald)
and that **SCARY GUY**
is about to cry.

A **true champion** is about more than just being number one.

A true champion **leads with their heart,**

inspires,

and most of all,
they make *everyone*
feel like a winner.

All alone, Dad's feeling quite small.
He wishes he never left the couch.

Thankfully, he's got a good coach.
One that doesn't give up
and helps Dad meet any challenge.

But can Dad get out of this jam?

Flowers won't do.

High-fives are left hanging.

Nothing's working at all!

Kid Coach and Dad huddle-up,
and decide to try . . .

a sincere apology.

But is it enough?

Kid Coach reminds
Dad how far he's come.

Dad thinks back to his
humble couch potato beginnings,

and digs deep for one last **classic** Dad move . . .

Before they know it,
BIG GUYS are glad guys,
BAD GUYS feel good,
(bald guys are still bald)
and that **SCARY GUY** is all smiles.

Everyone is **slammin'** and **jammin'** again in the ring!

**Kid Coach
is so proud.**

From **couch potato** to
***true* champion,**
Dad's finally earned
these friend chips.

To Melissa, who makes me feel like a true champion every day,
and to our little Kid Coach for teaching me so much.

Copyright © 2020 by Rob Justus

First published in 2020 by Page Street Kids,
an imprint of
Page Street Publishing Co.
27 Congress Street, Suite 105
Salem, MA 01970
www.pagestreetpublishing.com

Distributed by Macmillan, sales in Canada by The Canadian Manda Group

19 20 21 22 23 CCO 5 4 3 2 1

ISBN-13: 978-1-62414-886-6
ISBN-10: 1-62414-886-7

CIP data for this book is available from the Library of Congress.

This book was typeset in Mikado.
The illustrations were done digitally.

Printed and bound in Shenzhen, Guangdong, China

Page Street Publishing uses only materials from suppliers who
are committed to responsible and sustainable forest management.

Page Street Publishing protects our planet by donating to nonprofits like The Trustees,
which focuses on local land conservation.